River Rose

and the
Magical Christmas

Kelly Clarkson

illustrated by Lucy Fleming

HARPER

An Imprint of HarperCollinsPublishers

River Rose and the Magical Christmas
Copyright © 2017 by River Rose, LLC

For information address HarperCollins Children's Books,
a division of HarperCollins Publishers, 195 Broadway, New York, NY 10007.
www.harpercollinschildrens.com

ISBN 978-0-06-269764-6 (hardcover edition)
ISBN 978-0-06-279724-7 (special edition)
ISBN 978-0-06-274098-4 (signed edition)

The artist used ink, paint, and collage to create the illustrations for this book.
17 18 19 20 21   PC   10 9 8 7 6 5 4 3 2 1
❖
First Edition

To my amazing little unicorn children. Keep being bold! Keep laughing! And above all, please take care of me when I'm old—ha!
—K.C.

River Rose's favorite night was always Christmas Eve.
She knew Santa would stop by because she did believe.

To Santa

ELVES

River Rose and her dog, Joplin, had written him a letter.
And they were waiting up for him—hand-delivered would be better.

But River Rose and Joplin
accidentally fell asleep.

When she woke, she grabbed the letter
and ran downstairs without a peep.

River Rose and Joplin missed Santa but were surprised
to find above the fire three balloons they recognized.

These balloons were magical; they would take her on a flight above the mountains, through the clouds, past the moon that lit the night.

But as she wobbled, bounced, and swayed,
her hands clutched 'round the strings,
faintly through the silence she heard voices start to sing.

She followed the song to the North Pole, to a little village square.

She knew that this was Santa's home because elves were everywhere!

And there they sang:

Only a wish,
only a star,
only a leap
from where you are
for those who believe
on Christmas Eve.

Mrs. Claus appeared and said, "Santa will soon be back.
Until then, come in; please enjoy a North Pole snack!"

"One giant snowball fight—with snowballs you can eat!
Take a taste. You'll be surprised—each one will be a treat!

Or two rainbow lollipops—each lick will change your color."

River Rose was purple, then pink, then green as a four-leaf clover!

"Three chocolate trains that make you whistle with each bite!
Four colossal cookies to make you laugh and laugh all night!"

"Five jumping jelly beans will have you dancing around the room!

Six crazy candy canes you can fly up to the moon!"

"Seven golden eggs so delicious you will glow!

Eight tiny pies that make your body grow and grow!"

"Nine gingerbread houses to keep
you warm all throughout the night.

Ten warm cups of cocoa before we turn off the light."

Joplin fell asleep, and River Rose was fading fast.

As her eyes began to close, Santa came back at last.

He picked her up so gently and placed her on his sled.

"I think it's best, Ms. River Rose, if you sleep in your own bed."

She handed the letter up to Santa as he gently tucked her in.
Santa opened it carefully and grinned the biggest grin.

In all the letters he'd received, children from everywhere
were asking for a doll, a toy, a bike, or a teddy bear.
All were presents River Rose could have asked for, too;
instead the only thing she'd written were just the words "Thank you!"

When she woke Christmas morning, she wondered, was it a dream?
The snowball fights, the candy trains: was it really what it seemed?

She ran downstairs and there she found sitting beneath the tree
a music box for River Rose with a little golden key.

When River Rose turned the key, she knew it all was true.

Because the only ones who know that song are the elves, and me, and you.